MAGIC CANDIES

By **Heena Baek**

Translated by
Sophie Bowman

amazon **crossing kids**

I play on my own.

It's not all that bad, playing alone.
The other kids don't realize how much fun playing with marbles is.
They always only play with one another, never with me.
So I decided I'll just play by myself.

I need some new marbles.

Oh! I've never seen marbles like these before.
"Those are hard candies. They're very sweet,"
said the shopkeeper.
Ah, that makes sense. They're all different colors
and shapes and sizes.

Which one should I try first?
This pattern looks very familiar.

Wow, it's so minty I can feel cold air coming out of my ears!

All of a sudden I heard a strange sound coming from the living room.

Tong...
Tong Tong
Tong Tong
Hey, Tong Tong...

Over here...

Here... he

Gulp.
I swallowed.
And after that I could
hear it even more clearly.

Hey, Tong Tong. It's me, Sofa, . . .
your house sofa . . .

The remo . . . the remote,
it's . . . it's stuck in my side . . .

It hurts.

Ouch . . . ow!

Ow . . .

It's the sofa! The sofa's talking!

That's where the remote control is?

We've been looking all over for it since last Sunday.

Dad even got angry at me, saying I didn't put it back in its place.

I worked up all my courage and went over to the sofa.

That's it, that's it . . . Now there's just one more thing I have to say . . .

I need you to tell your dad to give the farting a rest . . .

I can't take it . . . the . . . the stink . . .

Tell him . . .

please . . .

don't sit here . . .

sit here and . . .

and fart . . .

Gulp.

When the candy in my mouth had all melted away, the voice was gone too.

This candy is really strange!

I wonder . . .

I knew it!

"What's that?"

"Then why do you keep running off?"

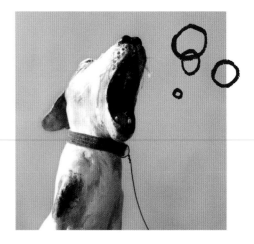

"Oh, now I get it. It's because playing with me is boring, isn't it?"

"Really? Then why are you always avoiding me?"

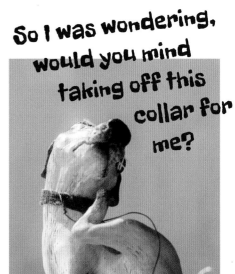

"Ah, I see. I'm sorry for dragging you around everywhere."

"Sure, why not?"

I've lived with Marbles for eight years, but today was the first time we ever got to have a conversation.

We played together all afternoon.

"Tong Tong! I'm home!"

It's Dad!

DID YOU DO YOUR HOMEWORK? CLEAN UP ALL YOUR TOYS. YOU CALL THIS CLEAN? CLEAN UP QUICKLY AND DO YOUR HOMEWORK. DID YOU WALK MARBLES? DID YOU PICK UP HIS POOP PROPERLY? DID YOU TAKE A PLASTIC BAG WITH YOU WHEN YOU WENT OUT? DID YOU WASH YOUR HANDS? IF YOU AREN'T GOING TO TAKE CARE OF HIM YOU HAVE NO RIGHT TO HAVE A DOG. WHAT'S WITH THIS HANDWRITING? WHAT A MESS. DID YOU FIND YOUR BIKE KEY? DID YOU WRITE YOUR NAME ON IT? WHAT ABOUT THE REMOTE? SIT UP STRAIGHT. DON'T SPILL YOUR FOOD. FINISH WHAT YOU'RE EATING BEFORE YOU GO OFF TO USE THE BATHROOM. MAKE SURE YOU SHUT THE DOOR. STRAIGHTEN YOUR BACK AND PULL YOUR CHAIR RIGHT UP TO THE TABLE. EAT SOME VEGETABLES TOO. CHEW PROPERLY. WITH YOUR MOUTH CLOSED. DID YOU WRITE DOWN ALL THE SCHOOL ANNOUNCEMENTS WORD-FOR-WORD AND BRING THEM HOME? DON'T DRINK WATER UNTIL YOU'RE DONE EATING. DON'T TALK WITH YOUR MOUTH FULL. IF THERE'S A LETTER FROM SCHOOL, LEAVE IT ON THE KITCHEN TABLE. YOU HAVE TO EAT ALL THE DIFFERENT THINGS THEY GIVE YOU AT THE SCHOOL CAFETERIA. DON'T BITE YOUR FINGERNAILS. DID YOU FEED MARBLES? PUT DOWN SOME WATER TOO. WALK CAREFULLY, AND DON'T MAKE SO MUCH NOISE. SHOW ME YOUR WATER BOTTLE. WHY DIDN'T YOU DRINK ALL THE WATER? YOU WENT TO BED WITHOUT HAVING A SHOWER YESTERDAY TOO, DIDN'T YOU? MAKE SURE YOU SHOWER BEFORE BED TODAY. AND CHANGE INTO FRESH UNDERWEAR. DON'T LEAVE YOUR PANTS TURNED INSIDE OUT WHEN YOU TAKE THEM OFF. RINSE YOUR HAIR PROPERLY. ONLY USE A LITTLE BIT OF SHAMPOO. YOU'VE GOT SUDS BEHIND YOUR EARS. GO AND RINSE AGAIN. BRUSH YOUR TEETH. DID YOU FLOSS? BRUSH YOUR TEETH AGAIN. YOU KEEP COUGHING. GARGLE WITH MOUTHWASH TOO. DID YOU CHANGE YOUR UNDERPANTS? YOU CAN WEAR THE SAME PAJAMAS AS YESTERDAY. PUT YOUR DIRTY LAUNDRY IN THE BASKET. DID YOU PACK YOUR SCHOOLBAG? DOUBLE-CHECK WHAT YOU NEED FOR YOUR AFTER-SCHOOL ACTIVITIES. MAKE SURE TO PACK YOUR PLANNER AND ANNOUNCEMENTS BOOK. GET OUT THE GYM CLOTHES YOU'LL NEED TOMORROW. READ A BOOK. NO, NOT A COMIC BOOK. I CAN'T HEAR YOU. READ IT OUT LOUD AND CLEAR. YOU ONLY NEED TO USE ONE WATER CUP. ONCE YOU'RE DONE, GIVE IT A GOOD RINSE AND LEAVE IT UPSIDE DOWN. YOU CAN'T EAT ANYTHING BEFORE YOU GO TO SLEEP. BRUSH YOUR TEETH AGAIN. WEAR A SWEATER TO BED. IT'S COLD. IT'S NINE O'CLOCK. QUICK, OFF TO BED.

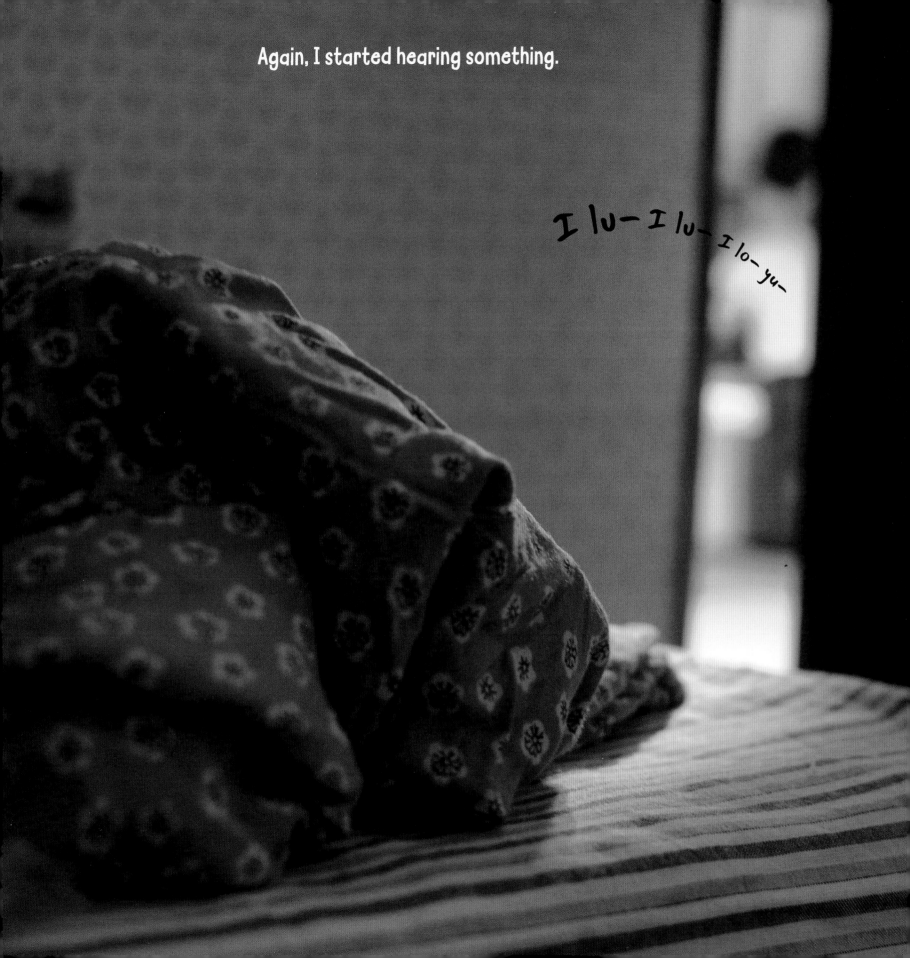

I love you

I love you

I love you I love you I love you I love you I love you I love you I love you I love you I love you

"Me too . . ."

I've only got a few candies left.
There isn't much that's pink in my life.

I wonder whose voice I'll hear this time.

Oh, it's soft. And there's gum inside. It's bubble gum!

I blew a bubble, and it flew straight out the window.

A while later it came floating back and popped. Right next to my ear.

It's Grandma's voice!

"Can you really hear me, Grandma?" I blew a big bubble and sent it off.

The bubble came back. *Pop!*

Oh, yes, I can hear you perfectly. Don't worry about me. I'm having so much fun here. I've been reunited with all my friends. We run around playing just like we did in the old days. I hope you're playing with your friends too, Tong Tong. Run around and play as much as you can.

I rolled the bubble gum into a neat ball
and stuck it under the kitchen table.

Now I can talk to Grandma
any time I want.

With this candy . . .

. . . the sound came from outside.

The very last candy, the see-through one,
was totally quiet no matter how much I sucked on it.

And so . . . I decided I might as well speak first.
"Do you want to play with me?"

With my thanks to Hongbi
for giving me endless inspiration
and Beomjun for supplying me with
all different kinds of marbles.

Previously published as *Alsatang* by Bear Books Inc. in South Korea in 2017.
Represented by Creative Authors Ltd. and Arui SHIN Agency.
Translated from Korean by Sophie Bowman. First published in English by
Amazon Crossing Kids in collaboration with Amazon Crossing in 2021.

Published by Amazon Crossing Kids, New York,
in collaboration with Amazon Crossing

www.apub.com

Amazon, Amazon Crossing, and all related logos are
trademarks of Amazon.com, Inc., or its affiliates.

ISBN-13: 9781542029599 (hardcover)
ISBN-10: 1542029597 (hardcover)

The illustrations were rendered in mixed media,
including handmade miniature figurines and environments.

Book design by Abby Dening
Printed in China

First Edition

10 9 8 7 6 5 4 3 2 1